POEMS for MARY

By

Ian McDonald

MiddleRoad | Publishers

www.middleroadpublishers.ca

Making Literature See The Light Of Day

OTHER BOOKS BY IAN McDONALD

FICTION

- The Hummingbird Tree (1969)

POETRY

- Mercy Ward (1988)
- Essequibo (1992)
- Jaffo The Calypsonian (1994)
- Between Silence And Silence (2003)
- The Comfort Of All Things (2012
- River Dancer (2016)
- People Of Guyana (with Peter Jailall) (2018)
- New and Collected Poems (2018)

DRAMA

- Tramping Man (1969)

NON-FICTION

- A Cloud Of Witnesses (2012)
- A Love Of Poetry (2013)

EDITED

- Selected Poems of Martin Carter (1989)
- Collected Poems of A.J. Seymour (with J. de Weever) (2000)

ANTHOLOGY (with Stewart Brown)

- The Bowling Was Super Fine — West Indian Cricket Writing (2012)

POEMS for MARY

Library and Archives Canada Cataloguing in Publication

ISBN 978-1-9991365-6-7 (softcover)

Cover photographs

Garden Painting by Merlene Ellis

Photo of Mary by Ian McDonald

Cover Design by Ken Puddicombe

POEMS for MARY

by Ian McDonald

"Rejoice in the things that are present; all else is beyond thee."

Michel de Monjaigne (1533-1592)

DEDICATION

For my wife

Mary

With Love

ACKNOWLEDGMENT

I express my gratitude to those who published these poems previously.

Most of these poems were published by Peepal Tree Press in the *New and Collected Poems of Ian McDonald*.

The Garden Poems first appeared in *The Comfort Of All Things* published by the Moray House Trust.

I am grateful to Ken Puddicombe and Middle Road Publishers for so promptly and efficiently getting *Poems For Mary* published. I admire the work Ken has done so willingly.

My sister Robin McDonald has been very helpful to me in preparing this book. I am grateful to her for her willing and creative support when so much needed.

Table of Contents

Poems for Mary

Preface To The Poems

In introducing a collection of my poems titled "River Dancer" I wrote the following about my wife Mary which I am content to reprint here as I reflect on our life together:

"Vibrant young woman came late into my aimless world. She has for very long been a large part of my life. How does one convey in life what plainly means nearly everything? What would a red thing be without the red? Length and breadth without the depth? We say to each other like children "I will love you forever".

That is true and that truth in my life has informed much of the poetry I have written even when the poetry is not specifically about Mary. Yet many poems have been directly inspired by her and this book contains them.

I was 46 and she was 29 when I got to know Mary and realized that she made life a lot more worth while. Since that time I have written poems for her, about her, with her in mind and situations in which her presence was deeply felt.

I have collected such poems in this book for her 70th birthday as a mark of love and honour for a beautiful and loving person who has anchored and protected and enhanced my life.
Ian McDonald

Ian McDonald

In The Essequibo

Poems for Mary

1. The Matchbox

A small girl, smaller than her age in years,

eyes astonished at the window ablaze,

the star-strewn tree, gifts glittering, haul of toys,

dolls so beautiful, dressed in lovely lace,

heaven-fall of pleasure, moves her hand,

touches the cold and bitter glass. In the other,

a little box is clutched — matchbox painted red

her mother made for her, tied with gold thread

to make it special. It is what she had

and she'll get nothing more except this visit

to the shining windows in the night.

Now beneath our tree, full garlanded and lit,

the grandchildren play in tangled toy-land glory,

be-ribboned merchandise stuffed in Santa socks,

their shining eyes darting here and there —

what they love best they hardly know,

happy in the rubbish of bright wrappings;

discarded boxes — *what else, what else to open?*

On this enchanted day, what else, what else to see?

Faded picture of a solemn girl, matchbox —

you can just see the golden thread —

held tight tight against her breast,

preserved against all fading Christmases, long ago.

Ian McDonald

2. *Wild Horses*

She remembers wild horses in the morning,
slim-child, walking miles to school.
She remembers early light above the cane field,
what the light does in the morning.
she walks between them on the stony path,
coats burnished by the rising sun
one wilder than the rest rises up,
stamps his metalled hooves down hard.
She fears them, fears him most of all,
passes them — no other path to take.
What fearsome thoughts possess their turning heads?
She passes them but does not run.
They toss their heads, their eyes are bright.

She dreams their dancing steps,
their glaring eyes bigger than the stars of morning.
Weeks go by; she walks by them in peace,
the demons faded in her mind.
She thinks they greet her, ducking down their heads.
Now she lingers before she passes on,
moves among them feels their trembling,
their coats ablaze with morning light.
She dares to face their shining eyes,

feel their power with her touch.

One morning they were gone for good

an empty path, an emptiness.

All her life she remembers.

Who would not be a tamer of wild horses?

Ian McDonald

3. The Struggle

Dark night on the river, water agleam,

moon climbing the storm-black stairs of heaven,

her sudden shout: *Got a tiger on the line,*

big big one, cannot handle, help me here!

But it is yours, you caught it good and strong.

You will not own it if you bring it in with help.

She doesn't answer; she struggles in the river,

knee-deep in moon-water churning,

the tiger pulling her this way and that,

shoulder joint wrenched out of line

her cry says the pain must be intense.

Remorseful, I go to help her. *No no no no*

I've got it. The fight goes on and on

and the rod bends to breaking,

but she knows the exact time to relax it.

Gradually she beats the great fish on the line;

strong and dangerous, but it lost her.

She brings it thrashing on the spit of sand,

hand-palm blister-bloody at the grip.

Moon was higher now, great tiger-fish gleaming,

thumping at her feet, standing skin-soaked,

gloriously small and pretty. I go to hug her.

Sorry, are you hurt, my love?

Poems for Mary

No you were right, of course. Why did I ask?

I think she's thinking of the long long years

I know the look. Her eyes are bright with victory.

Ian McDonald

4. The Starching Iron

Fatherless for so long, nine children

and a mother fending for bare bones of life,

food just enough and sometimes not,

cramped shelter and recycled clothes,

and something must be left for school.

In the market place from morning light,

the mother weary all the time,

eldest daughter nine years old

shares interminable chore of starching irons,'

a little wetting, sprinkled starch,

pressing neat the shirts and cricket-whites

and singlets patched and patched

and patched to use again.

We go out now to grand occasions,

my wife lovely in her party dress.

I pause in front the standing mirror,

see how perfectly my blue shirt falls

smooth and shining, no crease nor crimp.

I turn and hold tight her hand in mine,

tell her how beautiful she is.

5. *Star Of Love*

*('At this time of the year in the early hours of the morning,
Venus can be seen at its brightest in the Eastern sky'*

1988 Almanack: The sky at Night for December)

My son cries out

and I am up to see him

the sky is dark,

sea-wind blows in the rain;

there it blazes in the Eastern heavens,

the star of Love riding in the clouds alone,

gold ember burning tiger-bright.

memory flies back

when I too was young

my mother pointing

when I woke in tears,

voice gentle as a shepherd's flute:

'That is Christ's star,

Star of love, my son.

It brings beauty to the earth,

Blesses all of us.'

now as I comfort him

I point again to the great star

blazing in the Eastern heavens;

my son looks in a wonder

Ian McDonald

that dries

the tears in him,

and though the night is dark

and the hard rain blows in

my heart is filled again

with hope, the promise

that has lasted centuries.

'What is it?' my wife whispers,

our new child heavy in her.

'The Star of Love,' I say

'The Christmas Star, my love.'

6. *Praise Song For Mary*

Rounded

O of love

boon of heaven

heavy-looking now

birth soon to come

I celebrate the joy

beauty of body-swell

oval paradisal

proud miracle

I celebrate

all soft and circling forms

earth-root flower

the golden pregnant moon

showers shadows

call-glory of carols

bowls of ripe oranges

rose mangoes full plums too

stuffed sweet melons

rotund sun-ball in the sky

fat cloud-bellies sailing

in looms and loops of light

smoke-mist over water

rain curves on river

Ian McDonald

ocean-swoops billows

roses pools of moon-water

home home home

hollows look hallowed

they are the kin of hoops

fat loaves -

hot bounty

from old stoves

noontime and swallows

arcs of light

you are buoyant with becoming

a fountain

a meteor shower

flower-bloom

my burgeoning love

rock and cradling stars

in your belly-dark

time booms

and throb and towers

life starts again

I hear the double-heart

that God made with me

and you will make me soon

a high-shining son.

7. The Silver Brooch

My wife does not catch me looking at her;

she is combing out her hair, pinning it with

a silver brooch, putting on lipstick, bougainvillea red;

she appraised herself, she seems half-satisfied.

I think she should stop now. She is beautiful enough.

She pins the brooch another way. I see what she means.

Every moment of life I love her more. I go away

without her seeing me, to wait until she is perfection.

8. Flowers For The Home

Another time I watched her cutting flowers,
how she leaned low sometimes with the grace
women have. She looked so young. Watched
how she looked for the best, no clipping
in bunches, looked at each hibiscus, rose,
sunflower, orchid, matching in her mind
vases for our breakfast room.

9. *How My Son Was Born*

(My wife remembers)

Seven weeks early, two weeks more to put

on weight for safety that he needed;

suddenly he is there, insisted to be born.

Terrible pain. No, no, too soon, not now;

trauma will be too much for him.

"Prepare quick, we must take him out."

Desperate tension, young nurse hugging me,

steel tray falls — a brute and cruel sound.

I feel a barrel rolling, tumbling out.

He came in bursts of helpless pain,

my emptying womb, my rising fear.

Forceps in hand, the doctor caught him,

so small, crumpled, no hair, no nails.

What's in this world that will defend him?

Agony feeling he'll die, he's not alive.

He does not cry. No breath, he has no breath.

Nor can I breathe. Try, try, they tap him.

He will not cry. I see his face forever.

My son he will not try. They take him,

guard him from my sight. He will not cry.

I tell him with all my fervent heart,

Try, my son, try try. He cries, he begins to cry.

Ian McDonald

10. THE Almond Tree

Beneath this old beloved tree I sit and rest,
golden leaves falling from its shadowed green,
beautiful shining in the setting sun.
I am alone; tea brewed perfectly, salmon cakes
crisply made an hour past and pepper-seasoned
to my taste. A book I've brought with me.
The wind is sweet and cool; aloft the branches sway.
I do not see how I could be more content.
The book is Pascal. He tells me a little earth
is thrown upon one's head and that's the end forever,
thud of dirt thrown in an open grave.

My wife, granddaughter to look after,
joins me late. Smiling in the telling,
The bright child, she said as her hair was combed,
'You're shining me, Grandma.' Yes, my shining one,
That's so lovely. She sits beside me now;
thirty years we have spent such afternoons together;
the woodpecker chatters; hawks hang in the air;
hummingbirds gleam amidst the orchard vines.
Almond tree has grown from when she planted it;
green canopy now gives us this shadowed ease,
embraced by growing beauty through the years.

Poems for Mary

Night comes on, dousing red embers in the sky;

the white hare chases down the sloping field of heaven;

the spaces between the stars don't frighten me.

- 17 -

Ian McDonald

11. What It Was Like Once Forever

I wake to see the gleaming salmon

spring in the dark river of the morning,

the wind full of sea-salt and garden-flower,

the trees brimming slowly with green.

Mongoose, snake-catcher, sleek as a seal,

darts out of sight; I give him a sharp salute.

The day goes well. People are well-disposed,

what is owed to business is efficiently transacted.

Back home I leap heavenwards as high as I can,

Not far, but bravely done. My wife smiles,

she shakes her head, after all I am close to seventy-five.

There is no limit to our love,

even death will set no limit.

Our sons are content, healthy as snorting horses;

they will be coming soon.

I write this absurdly happy verse

to tell what it was like once, forever.

12. Gifts

I was coming home from the office;

it had been quite a good day —

finished a paper on markets overseas,

selling sacks of speciality muscovado

in the islands — good profit margin;

decided to bring home gifts for my wife,

not a birthday, not an anniversary,

just a sudden thought; why not?

I love her. She is good to me every day.

A simple dark-blue ceramic bowl,

red anthurium lilies in an earthen pot,

a wrap of green cloth with silver threads,

I loved this one, imagining it around her.

All this may seem extravagant, so many

sudden gifts, a whim. But what's

proportionate in the measurement of love?

I ran upstairs to bring them to her,

and she was astonished and hugged me

warm and close. *No, you shouldn't have.*

No, what is this? The cost, why now?

No explanation. She used the gifts right there:

red lilies near the place we always sit,

threw the green wrap around her neck

twirled to show me how lovely she found it.

joyously my gifts were gifted back to me.

Poems for Mary

13. Unwritten Diary

Between the pages of a diary left unwritten,

decades old, I find such keepsakes as stamps

I must have thought were valuable. Bourda Test card,

TIGER scrawled in capitals, photograph of farewell:

I count the faces — five died out of ten. Who will be next?

Note to myself I must have forgotten:

Check the children's vaccination (exclamation mark);

a page of cash transactions no longer making sense;

lists of books for ordering, urgently, it says:

Frost's *Collected Poems,* Wodehouse's *Gardens of the World*

for Mary. Yes, I remember how she hugged me;

sister's postcard from Hodges Bay Antigua,

telling me the laughing gulls have come again,

how my father used to say, *It's Ian's birthday then;*

advertisement for an antique Irish pendant

a-spark with jewels — but I never bought it;

invitation to an evening of dub poetry — I recall it -

there were drums, Ras Michael's eyes were bright;

wine list with the Madeira twice underlined,

from Miles — his word was law on horses, jazz and drink;

linked to lines I wrote and kept the scrap;

New Yorker cover — a splendour of peacocks;

most of all empty pages. What happened to my life?

Yes, notes from Mary with simple lines of love.

Ian McDonald

14. Routines

How important they are in this life which has an end:
keep the salt in the salt cellars flowing easily,
fill the morning vases with fresh and dewy flowers,
chilled water in the red-clay pitchers, shoes polished
to a Sunday shine, day's laundry fresh and folded,
replace the cake of soap before it's half a nub,
carefully sweep under the bright carpets,
take down the curious ornaments to clean each one —
chores that could regularly be skipped —
such things not really noticed if not done.
My wife goes out, says *See you later,* is gone.
I'm reading at my tidy desk. She stops, comes back,
gives my grizzled cheek a kiss.
There's something in being told I love you,
especially when you're not expecting it.

15. Forgotten In The Dance

Blessing of a quiet birthday at our pleasant home;

friends salute me with love and warm good wishes,

send bottles of good wine, one now joyfully shared

in the Orchid House; tinge of russet becoming night,

spices blowing in the wind. I say, *Come, love,*

let us dance a little. We fall into well-remembered steps,

as of old when we were courting.

Whisper to each other thousand-year-old clichés.

I've had my share of favours and good name.

How little it seems to matter now,

forgotten in the dance memories down the years.

Ian McDonald

16. Late Marigolds

Cold November wind flutters the last marigolds,
butterfly wings in the dark. Ah my love,
tears gather in my eyes thinking of when youth
was sweet in our limbs. Your dark eyes turn to me
giving permission. Forty years gone, unforgotten.
old now, I remind you; grasping my hand you smile,
hearts beating, as I remember.

17. The Coverlet

I wake beside her in the night, air turned to cold,

the soft woven, old, red-flowered coverlet —

family bequeathed forty years gone by —

slipped down her body lightly clad, her arms

clasped around herself, her legs drawn up.

She looks lost, lonely in the cold night.

Adjust the cover carefully as I can.

She stirs and murmurs, tense limbs relax.

Thank you, my husband, I am safe again.

Sighs, falls asleep. Enough, it is enough.

Ian McDonald

18. Smell Of Basil

I wander about in great contentment, watch her dig
the kitchen garden, great-boled tree undressing in the wind,
gold blossoms on the browning grass. Not far across
the ancient wall, high tide sends up leaping waves,
sea-froth scenting the garden air, mixing with the smell
of sunlight, black earth-dug with mould in beds.
She crumbles soil and sets the plants in place —
lettuce, pakchoi, peppers red and sweet. Half-barrels
sit in the big tree's shade filled with herbs she tends
with special care — parsley, thyme, rosemary, mint and dill —
she shows with pride their flourishing — sage and tarragon,
marjoram and bay. *Smell this.* She picks me leaves of basil
scrunched between her fingers at my nose.
Years, years ago, still sharp and green.

19. Poetry

Shimmering cloth, green and gold,

in two hours she knits a scarf,

every now and then she shows me

her work unfolding perfectly,

every movement poised and deft.

Line after line repeats her art,

astonishing how quick her fingers dart.

I sit beside her reading poems,

fine lines I love to read to her.

Don't, she says, *don't. I'll drop stitches.*

Be calm, be calm, you agitate my mind.

*A*nd so I mark the lines, for when she's done:

Carver's Fragment, Walcott's egrets,

Jeffers' passion for his dying wife in Hungerfield,

whose sprawling lines obsess me.

Sipping El Dorado and black Jamaican coffee,

fifteen year old liquor warms the heart.

She warms it to. The glittering scarf unfolds;

she holds it up complete. *For you when winter*

comes, she says. *Now read me your poetry, love.*

Ian McDonald

20. Gone To Get Ribbons

Ah my beloved, my rare beauty,

my heart fire, how I have loved you.

Without you I am lost.

Do not die, I pray, I am selfish, do not die.

Heaven protect me from the worst thing

to be the witness of your death.

I cannot sensibly exist if you do not exist,

darkness would come upon me worse than death.

No more to see yours eyes alight with life,

no more to feel the calm comfort of your arms

which once with such sweet passion embraced me,

no more to hear the way you sing when you

think no one s listening — I smiling in

the other room — no more of that:

I cannot bear to think of such desolations.

You went out this morning to buy fruits,

get ribbons for our granddaughter's hair.

Back soon! In a hurry you kissed me, touch-quick.

Wait, wait wait — putting out my hand.

Gone with a look back, knife sliced my gut.

I got up distracted, rattled pearls in my lucky-box.

21. Toasting The Moon

Once in my fine clothes, returning from a party feeling good,
I drank wine alone in our quiet moonlit garden
full of sleeping flowers, green trees black against the glow,
fragrant, singing, silvered dark. Lifted my wine to the moon
sailing in cloud, my heart bursting with the joy of love,
the shadow of my hand. My wife called, *Where are you?*
I'm toasting the moon, come down come down.
We danced under the moon and jostling stars.

Ian McDonald

22. Valentine

you never hold your love in check
or save it for some special time
you know love always is appropriate
filled and filling the hours of our lives
unstinted balancing reliable and sweet
the strong beat of your heart is mine
when I have need to be assured and centred
it is not only desperate times however
when you are there of course you're there
when death comes sure you'll be near
make that hard thing easier to bear I'll hold you
river-moon we loved you'll remind me
but what also is so true of love
as grass is watered the soul's small nourishments
you've brought up orchids near the table
where I've got used to read my books
and now darting out the kitchen smiling
try this roasted breadfruit hot with butter
and I've spent this morning a delightful hour
as you bathed and dressed our little granddaughter
combed her hair and ribboned it so apt and pretty
and that song you sing lights her up with joy

23. Essequibo Anniversary

eyes are sadder not too sad

bad days naturally mostly good

each knows each other's heart by heart

with death great loneliness will come

so little time has passed

years have flown like fallen leaves

hawks filled heaven's light that day

now a cloudless moon's vast light

carpets again this marvellous river

wind makes curls of silver brightness

silent we turn to one another

Ian McDonald

24. How Handsome You Look

Age fetters as surely as iron cuffs, hog-ties
the arms, legs, sinews to a felon's walk —
this slow decline from supple youth, light of foot,
turning on a penny, ardent every move
in course of games and love. Straight grows crooked
into hunch, light entering eyes grows dull,
every inch a hero becomes a joke. Who then
prays for more of time's dreaded work?
A mind lit by lighting and the world it still
can savour: birds over the shining river,
radiant in their homing flight this stranger
with a tale to tell — talks wildly all the night;
growing a good crop of garden vegetables,
and the woman I have loved so many years —
her smile delights me. She trims my hair, says,
How handsome you look! Who would not miss
the children laughing as they rush towards your arms?
Add it all up, it's life; we cling to it
despite the body finished by the years.

25. Moon In Old Age

A night full of beauty, moon ascending

in a scarf of cloud, throwing nets of light

to catch the huge whale of the river. Came here

in a lonely boat, an old man with pain

in the gut, fearing this may mean death.

It is the same beauty so many years ago

when I sat with my sweet love, and we smiled,

drew close and said we would never forget.

26. 35th Anniversary

I found my wife crying.
What had happened, what sadness had come
upon her? Not long before I had embraced
her, said how much I loved her. *Life is good;*
you make it good, my love. Talked about our
children's children for a while and she smiled,
squeezed my hand by the kitchen door. *Join me*
in the garden when you are done; there's a poem
I want to read to you. She was late coming
to me, said, *I cannot bear the thought*
I grow cold as death, I cannot bear the thought
there will come a day…
I held her close, close as I could.

27. River Dancer

Night is cold, she has gone a while.

The white smoke of age gets in my eyes,

but still I see her as she always was,

young and fearless and I in love with her.

Dirt poor made childhood bare as bone,

made her strong. She enriched me.

I see her brushing her long long hair —

All these years I have seen that —

and tears come in my eyes, so young again,

calling out to me her joy in creation:

a sudden decoration of orchids on the old tree,

a bank of vegetables and table greens.

See where I've got the sweet herbs now.

When I had cancer, fifty days hard treatment,

half my strength gone, not much left to love,

every day, every single day, she was by my side.

There is a picture of her dancing by the river,

turning to smile at me, hair swaying past her waist.

Ian McDonald

28. Masterpiece

Today mid-morning in Mary's kitchen,

all the ingredients: branch of red cherries,

lettuce on a plate, wedge of yellow cheese,

shoulder of lamb, cutting board with bread,

jug of cold water, and lady in a flowering apron,

all it needs now is Matisse.

29. Pots

He tried spinning pots for a living, not well-
made pots, lopsided in different ways, splotches,
dribbles of bright colour down one side not the other,
patterning not at all well done. We gave him a chance.
He delivered pots slowly; trial and error
clearly shaped them, some really badly botched,
always strong though, balanced OK. One day
we looked at each other; something in the pots
We loved. Flowers looked good, rightly placed
in those strong, haphazard pots. He got better
and better making them, got more and more
business, corporate commissions, took on assistants.
He thanked us for giving him a start, proudly gave us
big discounts. How could we tell him flowers
lived best for us in those beautiful first pots.

Ian McDonald

30. Acts Of Kindness

Family visiting, cousins from the old days,
hadn't been back for forty years, refugees
from the bad days of nothing in the shops, fear
of always being below, no future for the children.
they with gifts, brought back memories.
then it was bare food my wife didn't have;
now it was a tablecloth wonderfully embroidered
and, for me, bottles of Niagara wine. They were lovely.
We gave them a good time, laughter and memories.
When they left, my wife lamented, *Not Enough.*
Next morning I found her in the garden
Preparing a big basket of lettuce, fruits, herbs,
bunches of flowers to send where they were staying
in Industry, where they had lived so long ago,
where my wife endured her sad memories.
I feel better, my wife said. *Kindness filled their lives.*

31. Her Tasks Done Well

she goes downstairs to gather flowers in the sun

she does not see that I am seeing her

such a lovely thing my world is calmed

slowly she goes from bed to bed getting flowers

choosing them carefully for colour and for beauty

humming to herself brushing back her hair

and now she bends and digs out tough weeds

puts them in a special bag for garden rubbish

ah look she screens her eyes to watch the parrots fly

she goes over to the herb beds growing separately

looking I see she has the scent of them

I myself can almost smell them breathing deeply

how good this is watching her in the flowers

digging out the tough weeds smelling the herbs

with separate baskets for flowers and herbs

then she sits in the shade of the Orchid House

a while she rests wind in the trees above her

she doesn't stay long she is always hard-working

her mother told her day after day never waste time

she is happy with what she has done I can see

wanting to come up fix the flowers pack the herbs

I'll greet her with golden apple juice well chilled

Ian McDonald

share some time look at the beauty of the flowers
she will not know how completely content I am
to have seen her pick the flowers gather the herbs
sit by herself a little while quiet looking happy
her tasks done well good things for those she loves
I do not think it matters how old the universe will ever be

32. Nightfall

this day so sweet

before night falls

let us love forever

until night falls

I've grown old

my night falls soon

I will leave you

far too soon

you know my love

it will not fail

without end, my love,

until night falls.

Ian McDonald

33. Zoey's Cake

relaxed reading about Gauguin and Van Gogh

in sun-drenched Arles creating masterpieces

steps away Zoey helps her grandmother

in the kitchen baking Zoey just aged six

jumping up and down wanting so much to help

of course you can do this do that

such excitement my beloved little granddaughter

climbing on the kitchen stool laughing with joy

her hand held to guide the electric mixer

and then the first sweet drops of essence in the mix

helped her hold the wooden spoon to stir

couldn't help smiling to see the happiness

the jumping the laughing that pure delight

put on this baking apron we're doing icing now

all the little sprinkles grandma the silver and the gold

yes my love we won't forget the silver and the gold

we're doing well Zoey this will be very good

my wife hugging her on the tall kitchen stool

Zoey laughing sheer dancing joy I'm helping

is it going to be the best best cake Grandma

it's going to be the best best cake anyone ever made

Zoey you helped me you truly helped me

her laughter and the dance for joy it lasts forever

Poems for Mary

I have lived a long life and I have known delight

left it very late to know this joyous perfect moment

Ian McDonald

34. The Sound Of Making Butter

Ram the yardman brought home

the frothing pails of milk

fresh as that morning's dew

soon I hear that soothing churn

of butter being made by hand

sweetest I have ever known

spread-thick on home-made bread

little boy I remember

the lovely sounds of peace

Antigua sea on holiday

the brave blue sound of waves

the high wind in the cedar trees

on stormy nights of thunder

my mother in the room next door

gently singing to herself

and I am safe forever

35. The Lemon Tree

here it is again the marvelous morning light

rain-washed air freshened by the breeze

I remember gold-eyed egrets standing in green fields

and here they are again after all these years

they have not stirred they share eternity with me

grass green and soft as gleaming river moss

I was not well atall I was near death

my love has brought me home again

one last time perhaps I have come out in the morning

and there the old beauty is thirty years have gone

the wind rises and I smell the jasmine flower

and I hear her say long long ago for you my love

I have planted a lemon tree there it is for you

thick-leaved now heavy-fruited sweet-blossomed

in our heaven it has grown time passes

but beauty does not pass and love does not

Ian McDonald

36. The Comforter

old as long marriage and furnishing of home

familiar as love and children come for hugging

bright orange comforter drying on the line

swinging in the evening wind I notice it

the setting sun makes a blazing background

sudden cloud-move wind-wave light-shift

sun-flag dances on the line afire

warmth-burst from its colour and its care

no tear will go unmended see that golden patch

bring it in bring it in it will be cold tonight

37. Bread

my wife is making bread

little girl in poverty she learnt

she is singing she is making bread

mixing the yeast the flour the art

adding in a soupcon of sugar her spices

kneading just right letting it rise perfectly

heaven's fragrance is the smell of baking bread

makes me pause my task breathe the very air

I've heard silk and gold are the best gifts

brings me small loaves cut and buttered on a plate

"bless you love" summary of a life

Ian McDonald

38. The Arrival Of Happiness

late morning rain coming down heavily

sky black-clouded horizon to horizon

not the sort of day for exaltations

there was an open-air jazz concert later

going to enjoy it cancelled of course

anyway wife bought us cups of coffee

the veranda green hanging ferns around us

orchids in a bowl Greaves painting we loved

two pure white egrets surprised us

flags waving past landed with a splash

stood loving the rain elegant garden artwork

rain the coffee wife there sudden beauty life

39. Camp-Fire

went to bed earlier than my wife

finishing touches to her cross-stitch pattern

listening contentedly to the music

Pavarotti ascending to where angels sing

I was cold went near her my camp-fire

put my hand out to touch her face

"love you" she said "love you too"

"sleep well until morning light" something she says

I don't anymore of course not the point

woke sometime later her dark hair

scattered wildly like I remember

Ian McDonald

40. Forecast

we are not what we fear we will become

not yet anyway not sad not sick not nothing

I have risen with birdsong strong and healthy

"for my age" as old men proudly claim

you have arranged the flowers made the coffee

we sit and talk about the day to come

old Cameron the gardener will bring his gold papaws

told us about his harvest with pleasure in his voice

we know the grand-children are visiting a great blessing

exchanging stories about them we laugh into each others' eyes

it's hard but we avoid the hate in headlines

there are so many ways to love this world

the time immediately ahead of us is very good

outside we will walk amidst the red blaze of poinsettias

there is the music of the wind in the tall trees

let me say the earth is giving a good account of itself

today and tomorrow and as long as we want to think

we can forget completely what the old priest's sermon said

all beauty raised on high will also be thrown down

41. "I Will Not Let You Die My Love"

for long the days darkened in my life

time comes when breath is hard to get

weakness stills the limbs effort makes no sense

world a-tilt wild colours in the head

she never failed my Northern Star my love

grasped her shoulder getting to the garden

one hundred song-birds in their beauty greet me

alighting in the quiet tree's green and golden branches

glimmering in the wind their gleaming wings

their throats of silver poured forth such music

I was moved to wonder and to tears of love

so good again to breathe sweet air and live

Ian McDonald

42. What We Want Of Love

So much we desire of love, so much:

that it be perfect, that it be absolute,

that it take us across astonishing gulfs

of danger and harm and hurt and fear,

that it heals all wounds inflicted by the world;

when we are young, that it be passionate,

set fire to the skies of day and night,

be honey on the bread of life,

a gleam of beauty always present,

that it should bear rich fruit.

But when the last comes, as it must,

all we want of love is narrowed down:

whom we love need not be glamorous or strong,

brave or exciting or providing everything;

what mattered once does not matter now.

Do not leave me leave me to the black night coming

be with me with me one day one hour

one more day one hour more be with me

one more hour one last hour forever.

43. The Last Dance

it is long long ago

forty-one years to be precise

I am now very old

she seems young to me

but she isn't I suppose

I remember the first time

first time I realized something

said to her at the party

I want the last dance

she said yes you can

I will always want the last dance

I said and she smiled

Ian McDonald

THE GARDEN POEMS

- 54 -

*"The garden created by Mary, my wife, over thirty years, is a
continual joy. These fragments have been clipped from her
creation."*

MARY'S GARDEN

As golden afternoon transmutes into silver evening and then into velvet darkness fretted by stars I sit to read and think and dream. It is a place of peace and beauty and therefore truths are very likely to be revealed. Where I am is the garden which my wife has created. God bless her and those who have helped her — Alston, Kenneth, Andy — for what she has quietly achieved over these many years. It is as much a work of art as a painting by a master spirit or a piece of perfect music by a composer connected to the spheres behind the radiant sun and the serenely floating moon. How fortunate I am to step from days of hurly-burly living and the often fractious tedium of coping with ordinary chores and life's sudden sink-holes into this haven of green peace and flowers in the wind. It is but a step indeed and life is transformed. How many possess such benefit for a life-long time? If you are a believer make a holy sign, if you do not believe then bow in gratitude for the favour great Nature has been pleased to bestow.

Sometimes, before I go to read, when the light from the sky is especially beautiful, I walk, book in hand, in the many spaces of the garden. I look up — a hawk soars from branch to branch sun flashing on its wings. I treasure everything I see. At certain times of the year the rush of blood in the flamboyants and at Christmas the fire-coal of poinsettias flame and glow. There are the sumptuous capes of purple orchids thrown across the arbour by the kitchen garden and fans of golden orchids blow along grey-mottled boughs. All about is hibiscus, the garden's glory, flowering anew every day. A vine of sky-blue blossoms half-cover a white wall, a curtain of heart-shaped leaves incomparably woven. Bougainvilleas sway and blaze in high hedges planted long ago. Everywhere repeating and repeating the signature of beauty. Once after rain in a sun-shimmering pool in a corner of the garden I saw two golden-eyed egrets motionless side by side ancient as Egyptian centuries. Give thanks for all that you are given to admire and to love.

Ian McDonald

The setting where I read is full of calm and grace. Near the white wooden chair in which I sit and which has come to fit my back so well a fountain plays in a pool circled by green ferns with banks of red ixora surmounted by frangipani of purest white. The sound of water falling into water ceaseless as a far sea is a background I have grown to love and when the sea-wind rises in the trees the sigh of branch and rustle of the leaves supplement and meld with the quiet conversation of the water in an extraordinary serenade of murmuring and restful sound. Later afternoon there is birdsong everywhere — the birds settling on the telephone wires like notation on a sheet of music. And as night comes on the small frogs begin their ricocheting ringing.

More raucous sounds at times obtrude. I sit beneath tall trees older than the garden and sometimes parrots come to screech and chatter in the branches overhead and, I swear, bombed me for fun with bits of bark and chewed almond seeds until I stand up and pelt them back and chase them squawking to another perch. When the sea-wind rises stronger the tree-boughs creak and branches crack. And at spring tides increasingly these days in fierce wind you can hear the wave-crash and the roar of the sea hovering ominously over the town.

But mostly the sounds of peace prevail. These sounds I have grown to love. So many years gone by. The sift and sigh of garden wind falling on the ear. My wife calling from the Orchid House, "Come see this love, come see this beauty!" The sounds of the garden over these more than score of years have forever entered the cells of memory and I can lie awake in cold winters in cities far away and I can hear them still.

The three parts of my life in the garden — reading, thinking, dreaming. Distinct and inseparable — the mind giving rise to wonders without limit. As I settle into my reading the mind, as Andrew Marvell in his celebrated poem says,

"Withdraws into its happiness;
The mind, that ocean where each kind
Does straight its own resemblance find;
Yet it creates, transcending these,

Poems for Mary

Far other worlds, and other seas,
Annihilating all that's made
To a green thought in a green shade."

Books — how they have made it so good to be alive. I cannot count the number of books I have read sitting in the white chair by the fern-wreathed fountain. Let the one I have been reading the past few days stand for them all: Sarah Bakewell's marvelous biography of Michel Eyquem de Montaigne. It has led me back to reading Montaigne's great essays. These in themselves are an entire education. In them Montaigne invented the art of reflecting humanity at large by writing about himself. If you want to judge for yourself get this book, subtitled How to Live, and also read Montaigne's "Of Experience", "How We Cry and Laugh for the Same Thing", "Of Friendship", How Our Mind Hinders Itself", to mention just four. Life freshens and is renewed and means more as you read his work. Montaigne believed that every moment has a purpose unto itself. As I read and think and dream and the garden surrounds me with a beauty which is different every day I can believe that. Every moment has a purpose unto itself. I should live like that.

On evenings when I sit in Mary's garden just as it is getting dark a humming-bird comes to hover and suck the honey-dew from the myriad flowers all around. It is never more than one hummingbird, I can't understand why. It cannot be the same humming-bird for more than twenty years but I have come to think it is. Under the skies of darkening red or deepening silver-blue or the last golden light of a perfect day it darts and shivers among the flowers as I watch. It has entranced me all these years. A very few times it has not come and I have been bereft and I have researched my day to see what harm or hurt I might have done. Nothing so beautiful as its brightness in the evening air — an incandescent blessing, incomparable intricacies of flight, a shimmering amid the green leaves. I am completely silent in wonder. It is the Spirit of the Garden. Long after I have gone I like to think it will be coming to gleam and hover among the flowers in the evening light. And perhaps our grandchildren, should they be so blessed, will in their turn gaze in wonder at its shimmering beauty.

Ian McDonald

GARDEN POEMS

The Great Trees

I doubt there is anything
more beautiful than the flying moon
between the branches of great trees
clouds obscuring
then revealing
leaf-entangled stars
night after night
the great trees stand.

Tree Orchids

sumptuous cape
of purple orchids
thrown overnight
across the boles
of mottled bark
flourish in the wind
wrap of kings.

Shower Of Gold

sun flags
fall among the leaves
sudden fans of gold
wind-waved
along black boughs

drip brightness
the old tree
radiant again

Flamboyant

gnarled tree
blackened branches
wind-awry
death coming
this year sure
sudden green filigree
bursts of red
rush of blood

Frangipani

intense colour
white without flaw
pennants flying
in the sun
spears aloft
amid the green
sharp white fragrance.

Ian McDonald

Almond

glossy green leaves
age to gold
lovely to read below
green overhang
where green parrots
hide and throw
bitten seeds down
look up delighted
shake my fist.

Water Coconut

cutlass on high
brings down the ripened fruit
lop its green head off
white pith and shell
sip sweet and cool
what God called water
scoop soft jelly
eat and live forever.

Rosemary And Thyme

crushed rosemary
chipped thyme
aromatic walk
daybreak sun
breathe deep
fresh morning air
in my pocket
a handful of fragrance.

Poems for Mary

Lime Tree

noon-blaze
this cooling place
lime laden branches
shelter me
what a blessing
cut limes
a sweetened pitcher
crack of ice.

Rose of Gold

pure gold could not
possess this gleam
sun enters
every sovereign bloom
leaves are dark
day is dark
these petals pull
all gold all light
to show us all
what gold is really like

Midnight Rose

rose bred
to such red darkness
blood of centuries

gathers at its heart
moon crescent gleams
above this bed
of wild black leaves
thorn and dark rose
a deeper shade
of night.

Night Choir

darkness descends
out of sky
out of earth
cacophony or silver
frog calls creak
crickets sing
lone cicada hums
throaty songs of night.

Garden Storm

tempest in the trees
a savage rain
wind-whipped flower-fall
it softly ends
silver patterning
and nothing greener
than drenched green.

Sea Wind

hot stillness ends
winds from the sea
murmurous and fragrant
hustle plants
toss the tops of trees
blossoms fall
leaves scatter on the grass
in dancing disarray.

Grass

new cut lawn
sun's oxygen
fill the lungs
breathe deep
again and again
smell of health
and homecoming.

Water Lily

soft evening light
sun dance of birds
they skip and peck
bright and joyous
leaf to leaf
green to green

Ian McDonald

float on silver
white blossoms
beneath their feet.

Water Hyacinth

such lithe growth
slithering green
alive as eels
bubbles bursting
and blossoming
this sun-tangled
frog-heaven
emerald abundance.

Bluebells

blue as eyes
sun bright
jewels strung
in a nymph's hair
sapphire sparks
bride's joy.

The White Chairs

two empty chairs
side by side
white in shadow
canopied by orchids

why do they
sadden me so?

The Orchid House

where we take tea
tasty meat patties
see the burnished sky departing
variously beautiful
are the humming-birds
come out at six o'clock
surrounded by flowers
and peace.

Ground Orchid

rare blossoming
garland of silver
dropped overnight
on the dark green
one day a year
and gone.

Lilies Of The Field

half a field
of beauty

blowing in the wind
white carpet
lustrous as Persia
age-old poetry
breaks my heart.

Fern

fountain's edge
fern tendrils
creep deep green
mosses underneath
slipperiness of rocks
water gleams
in the sun
blows in the wind
bright fan.

Fountain

green leaves drip
into clear cool water
Ixora bands of red
ring the quiet pond
spears of silver
arc and glisten
in the wind.

The Cassias

four cassias
mounting to heaven
give blessings' of their shade
yet April comes
they rain down sun.

Solace

news of a death
walk hand in hand
under whispering trees
amidst orchids
the colour of tears
the kindness of the garden.

Egrets

sun-shimmering ponds
of morning rain
gold-eyed egrets
motionless
side by side
old as centuries.

Ian McDonald

Bougainvillea

throw of red
against the wall
bougainvillea abloom
shouts of colour
joy of children
phagwah in the garden.

Marigolds

struck by Brilliance
intensity of gold
in a small space
no one looking
covered my face
in soft blooms
able to say
I bathed in marigold.

Hibiscus

garden's glory
hundreds all abloom
wind awakes them
I walk amidst
the fire of their colours
thanking and praising
my wife my beauty.

Hedges

hibiscus all aflame
crimson and soft ochre
patches of ixora red
and green ficus
creamed with white
years have built
these walls of peace.

Going Away

Where my life has been sweetly centred,
this garden is wildfire, sometimes hot and gold,
ripe-sun-lit blaze of flowers, sky aflame.
This evening colour calmed to mists of lightest blue;
I sit alone in this green and quiet place.
Over the sea wall, far-out grey clouds
merge with silver blush-smudged sea,
white-winged birds, pale shadows,
weave patterns in the darkening air.
Tomorrow I leave here for a while.
Fine drops of rain begin to fall. I won't move
until the hummingbirds appear,
bright jewels gleaming in the dying light,
branch of crystals shaking in the gloom.
When will I return? These days nothing is certain.

Ian McDonald

Born in Trinidad, West Indies, Ian was educated at Queens Royal College and Cambridge University. His career has spanned several decades in a variety of fields: Business, Sports and Literature. Ian is the recipient of Guyana's Golden Arrow Of Achievement. The University of the West Indies in 1997 awarded him honorary Doctorate Of Letters. He has been a Fellow of The Royal Society Of Literature since 1970. He has written extensively on cricket. In addition to writing poetry and prose, Ian has edited and co-edited numerous collections and anthologies. His novel *The Hummingbird Tree* (1969) was made into a BBC film. He won the Guyana Prize for Literature — Poetry, three times: in 1992, 2004 and 2012 and has published seven poetry collections in addition to short stories and two collections of essays and speeches. He continues to write on cricket and poetry and several publications are in the works.

Racing With The Rain

By Ken Puddicombe

Available on amazon

"Ken Puddicombe's brilliant novel…an historic political conflict in Guyana, during the Cold War and the cold cynicism and tragic irony of a state sacrificed to super-power hegemony." -Frank Birbalsingh, author of *Novels and The Nation: Essays in Canadian*

JUNTA

By Ken Puddicombe

Available on Amazon

"A gripping story (of) an imperfect democracy…the tension…builds increasingly from page to page."—Rico Downer, author of *There Once Was a Little England.*

Down Independence Boulevard And Other Stories

by Ken Puddicombe

Available on Amazon

"A brilliant collection of stories telling the tales of people forced to leave their homes…craving the past, escaping from racial conflicts and dictatorship…"—Judith Kopacsi Gelberger, author of *Heroes Don't Cry.*

Perfect Execution

by Michael Joll.

Available on Amazon.

"Michael Joll is a master of surprise endings, but they never seem forced. He always stays true to his characters and their worlds." —Nancy Kay Clark, author and editor, *CommuterLit.com*

Poems for Mary

Persons Of Interest

By Michael Joll

"Exotic and intriguing! Joll brilliantly captures the reader's interest with vivid imagery and a relentless sleuth." —Phyllis Humby, short story writer, poet and novelist.

Unfathomable And Other Poems

By Ken Puddicombe

"Reading Unfathomable…One is aware of the sounds, smells and music of the country…using structure and sound to take the reader into the poem." —Jennifer Footman, author of *St. Valentine's Day*

Witnesses

By Raymond Holmes

"Whether comedic or tragic, plunge his readers into vivid slightly askew worlds, where violins hold memories, suitcases vanish, ghosts abound and death waits behind every door."—Nancy Kay Clark, author of *The Prince of Sudland: Escape from the Palace.*